Mr. Bumble and the Hippo

a story for anyone who ever loved a pet

written by
Bill Wheatley

illustrated by
Jane Duderstadt

The Wooster Book Company
Wooster ▪ Ohio
2001

The Wooster Book Company
where minds and imaginations meet
205 West Liberty Street
Wooster Ohio • 44691
www.woosterbook.com
800-WUBOOK-1

ISBN 1-888683-10-4

Library of Congress Cataloging-In-Publication Data

Wheatley, Bill.
  Mr. Bumble and the hippo : a story for anyone who ever loved a pet / written by Bill Wheatley ;
    illustrated by Jane Duderstadt.
        p. cm.
    ISBN 1-888683-10-4 (alk. paper)
    1. Dogs—Fiction. 2. Pets—Death—Fiction. I. Title: Mister Bumble and the hippo. II. Duderstadt, Jane.

    PS3573.H412 M7 2001
    813'.6—dc21   00-068589

♾ This book is printed on acid-free paper that meets industry standards for permanency.

special thanks to:

Elizabeth Kodama
Patience Bundschuh
Candace Anderson
David Wiesenberg

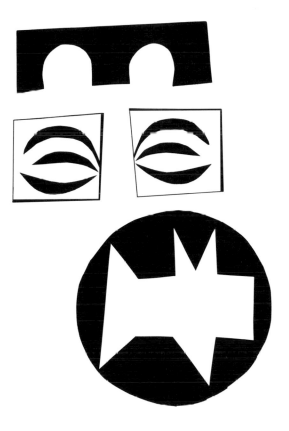

1. Mr Bumble and the Hippo

*M*r. Bumble was a small—a very small—golden-red dog. He got his name because of the way he buzzed and bumbled along on the end of the leash like a bee when he went for a walk with his mistress Jane.

She had long golden-red hair which was almost exactly—but not quite—the same color as his, and she always walked a little too fast. Although she had only two legs, they were both very long, and Mr. Bumble had to bumble along to keep up.

Every day his mistress Jane walked him and fed him and wiped off his paws when it was snowy or wet. She trimmed his hair when it grew too long for him to see through the tuft that curled over his eyes, and gave him a bath when he had a flea. She hugged him and kissed him too, a little more than he liked, and a little more than was necessary. But he didn't really mind because it made her so happy, and also because she gave him a biscuit to eat as a reward for putting up with so much affection.

When Mr. Bumble was young, he lived in the city where the sidewalks and tree trunks and fire hydrants were ripe with smells. They made his nose twitch with an urge to take long, lingering sniffs. But his mistress Jane was always in a hurry. After just one or two sniffs he felt a tug on the leash and she pulled him along, because they had to get home, or they had to cross the street to avoid the Galloping Galoot—a very large dog who never walked on a leash—or for no reason at all, except she wanted to go.

In the morning when she took him on the long walk to work, they passed a thousand things that needed to be sniffed. Not just tree trunks and fire hydrants, but incredible things like the dumpster overflowing with so many pizza boxes it made a dog dizzy just to whiff from a distance. Or half a ham sandwich lying right by the curb. But she yanked him away before he could bite it, and he never saw it again.

On their way to work they passed the building guarded by two giant stone cats, bigger than any dog he'd ever seen. But the cats never moved, not even when Mr. Bumble left a drop of water on each of their paws.

The city was full of dangerous threats to a terrier, his mistress Jane always reminded him. She pulled him close to her legs so he wouldn't get stepped on by jogging shoes, or run over by bicycles, or squashed under a bus. Everything was so much taller and bigger than him that sometimes Mr. Bumble was a little frightened himself, but he never let anyone know it.

They walked up the long hill, then down and over the bridge, to the old brick building filled with stairways. Inside Mr. Bumble bounded his short legs up one flight after another, past the Cat Who Wouldn't Be Sniffed, through the steel door, and into the room with tall windows.

This was his mistress Jane's studio and now they were at work.

Mr. Bumble curled up on the couch and did his job, which was to sleep for three or four hours, while his mistress Jane did her equally important job putting colored pieces of paper on cardboard. Whenever there was a noise in the street below, Mr. Bumble had to wake up, jump on the back of the old couch, and look out the window. All he could see was the sky, and rooftops, and some chimneys. He woofed a few times till the noise went away, jumped down, and curled up again.

Then it was time to go home. Down the long stairs, over the bridge, back up the hill, and then down.

Whenever they went for a walk, his mistress Jane always looked out for dogs, especially big dogs, the kind who might challenge Mr. Bumble's doghood just because he was so small.

As soon as they turned the corner toward their house, she picked him up, in case the Galloping Galoot was out patrolling the street. Tucked in her arms so high off the ground always made Mr. Bumble feel very undignified, and he had to bark fiercely so the Galoot wouldn't think he was scared.

If they saw Attila the Pit Bull leading the Smoking Lady down the sidewalk, his mistress Jane always yanked so hard on the leash that two or three of Mr. Bumble's feet left the ground. "Don't *ever* woof at Attila!" she warned him. "He could chomp you in two with one bite!"

The only big dog he was allowed to meet was Derek, who slept in front of the laundromat, and was so old he wheezed when he got up to sniff Mr. Bumble. Sometimes Derek didn't even bother to get up, but just opened one eye and closed it again without moving his head.

The few times he met someone his own size, his mistress Jane let them touch noses and sniff each other, and sometimes they played till their leashes got tangled. But there were very few dogs just the same size, and Mr. Bumble had never met anyone smaller than him in his life.

It was frustrating not to sniff other dogs, but Mr. Bumble had to admit that his mistress Jane might be right to protect the bigger ones from meeting him. If you were very small and very dignified, it was sometimes necessary to bite a large dog before he bit you, and that could lead to trouble.

When they got home, his mistress Jane hugged him and kissed him, and told him how much she loved him, and gave him a biscuit because he put up with so much affection. He was fond of her too and liked his life very much, even though she never let him sniff all the things that needed to be sniffed.

One day, instead of going for their long walk, his mistress Jane and her husband, Mr. Grumble, packed up everything in the house, loaded it into a big yellow truck, and moved to the country.

Suddenly, everything was quiet.

Suddenly, everything smelled different.

Mr. Bumble was in a new world. All the scents were so strange, he felt as if he had a new nose.

There were no sidewalks in the country and at first Mr. Bumble was afraid to leave his mark on the trees and rocks by the side of the road. He wasn't sure this was really his place. But no one told him he couldn't. So one day he did. And nothing happened. Then he began to leave his sign everywhere.

He heard new things too, not just the cawing crows and braying jays he'd heard in the city, but singing finches and whistling cardinals and jabbering grosbeaks. There were even flying dogs called geese that honked just like barking. Mr. Bumble tipped his head back and woofed at them, but they flew across the sky and disappeared.

There were many strange creatures in his new home.

Every morning at sunrise, Mr. Grumble walked him up the steep hill to the field, where the tall brown animals with white tails ran away as soon as he saw them. And the red dog with the long red tail—who wasn't really a dog at all—took a quick look at Mr. Bumble, jumped over the stone fence and vanished. The only strange creature who didn't run away was the strangest of all. He was covered with needles, and crossed the road very slowly right in front of them, as if they weren't even there. But Mr. Grumble warned Mr. Bumble that the needles were designed for one special purpose—to stick in dogs' noses. So he could never, ever, get close enough for a sniff.

It was disappointing not to meet any of the strange creatures, but there were plenty of other things to see and smell in the country when his mistress Jane took him out for their afternoon walk.

They went up through the village and out to Kate's farm, where the sheep came up to the fence and made a noise that sounded as if they didn't like anything, especially terriers.

They went down to Werner's Pond, where the peepers peeped louder than the Galloping Galoot ever barked.

They went up to the Lookout, where his mistress Jane looked at the beautiful view, and Mr. Bumble sniffed the footprints of squirrels on tree trunks and the holes in the ground the chipmunks disappeared into.

As he bumbled along on the end of the leash, she talked to him the same way she always did in the city. She still had to put colored pieces of paper on cardboard every day, whether she felt like it or not. And now she had a garden, with Brandywine tomatoes and Dragon Tongue beans and Pretty Purple Peppers. But it never got enough rain. Or else it got too much. And what was she going to cook for dinner? Her dinner, not Mr. Bumble's. His dinner was always the same.

She told him all the things she worried about, like the time her father got sick and he could tell without looking up she had tears in her eyes. Then he felt himself suddenly lifted off the ground and squeezed in her arms.

"Oh, Mr. Bumble," she said. "I hope you don't ever get sick! What would I do without you?"

To let her know he was feeling just fine, he licked her tears till her cheeks were dry. Then he wiggled, and she put him down, and they started home.

As peaceful as it was in the country, there were still threats to Mr. Bumble's doghood.

If they saw Tyrannosaurus Taurus, the mayor's rottweiler, taking himself for a walk in the village, his mistress Jane shouted, "Go home, meathead!" Then they hurried away, while Taurus tried to figure out who she was shouting at.

When they walked past the big house with the old red truck parked in front, the Murray Monster stuck his head out the window and barked ferociously. But he never jumped out, and his truck never went anywhere.

If they saw Commander Bark teetering down the road behind his twin chows, his mistress Jane pulled Mr. Bumble to one side until they passed by. Genghis and Tofu had long purple tongues and were always smiling at something.

When they passed the House of Many Woofs, where ten dogs and twenty cats all lived together, his mistress Jane only let Mr. Bumble sniff for a moment, because as soon as he did the whole house started woofing.

And when they got home, his mistress Jane hugged him and kissed him and told him how much she loved him. It was always a little embarrassing, even when he secretly liked it. But he was a pet, and that was his job—to walk and be talked to and hugged.

There was really only one thing wrong with Mr. Bumble's life in the country. He couldn't show his mistress Jane his own pet.

Mr. Bumble's pet was as big as Mr. Bumble was small. It was as dull gray as Mr. Bumble was bright golden-red, as smooth as his master was hairy, as rare as a terrier was ordinary.

Mr. Bumble's pet was a hippo.

He was proud of his pet and wanted to show him to his mistress Jane, but was afraid she might say his pet was too big—what if it rolled over and crushed him? Or she might say dogs didn't keep hippos as pets—nobody did—and there was even a law against it. So Mr. Bumble was wise enough to keep his pet secret.

But it was hard to keep something as big as a hippo a secret, so the only time Mr. Bumble took him out was when he was sleeping. Curled up on the bed or in his den underneath or on the gold couch in the living room, as soon as Mr. Bumble fell asleep, he took his hippo out for a walk.

Mr. Bumble held the leash in his teeth or around his paw, and as they walked down the road he let the hippo stop to sniff as often as he wished. Now and then he even stopped to sniff something himself, and the hippo didn't pull or tug but waited patiently till his master had marked the spot, and then they moved on.

When people saw Mr. Bumble walking his hippo, they stopped and said, "He's so beautiful—and so big! As big as a school bus! Can I pet him?"

"Yes, go ahead," said Mr. Bumble. "But be careful, he can be shy."

Everyone was impressed when they saw Mr. Bumble walking his hippo, most of all the other dogs.

When Genghis and Tofu saw a terrier leading his pet up the road, the twin chows yanked the Commander far over to the other side, and ran past with their purple tongues tucked tight in their jaws.

The Murray Monster ducked his head down inside the truck, so Mr. Bumble's pet wouldn't know he was there.

And when Tyrannosaurus Taurus saw Mr. Bumble with his great gray companion, he gave a meek little whimper and ran away. The sight of a dog walking his very own hippo was too much for him.

Now that Mr. Bumble was a master instead of a pet, every dog they passed stood respectfully staring, sniffing the air a good distance away.

For the first time in his life, Mr. Bumble didn't have to defend his doghood.

At first, having his own pet to take out for walks was an adventure, something exciting and different to do. But after a while—and it wasn't very long—Mr. Bumble realized it was not only fun having a pet, he was beginning to care about him too, and even worry about whether he was all right.

What if he lost his hippo, he wondered, or if the hippo got sick? Mr. Bumble began to feel that he couldn't get along without his pet. But whenever he went to sleep the hippo was there waiting for him, ready to go out for a walk, and he rumbled along so happily that Mr. Bumble started calling him Mr. Rumble.

The two of them bumbled and rumbled along together, and whenever Mr. Rumble wanted a treat, he nudged Mr. Bumble with his huge nose and opened his mouth as wide as a yawn. Then Mr. Bumble carefully set a cabbage on the long pink carpet between teeth the size of tree stumps and watched as the jaws closed like a trunk lid. Cabbages were just like dog biscuits to Mr. Rumble and he couldn't get enough of them. He always knew just how many Mr. Bumble had brought along too, so that was how Mr. Bumble learned his hippo was smart enough to count, which made his master very proud.

Mr. Bumble took his hippo everywhere during their walks, places he had never gone with his mistress Jane but always wished he could visit.

They found the place where dog biscuits fell from the sky and cabbages were piled up like snowdrifts, and they both ate till their bellies were stretched tight as balloons.

They discovered an endless soft green lawn where leaves were always falling and blowing and twirling around, and Mr. Bumble taught Mr. Rumble how to chase them, though he wasn't very good at it. Whenever he tried to stop short, his huge legs sank into the turf so far he had trouble pulling them out, and when he turned too quickly, he rolled over on his side and made a little ravine in the meadow.

One time they found a freshly raked garden where Mr. Bumble dug a big hole with his paws and Mr. Rumble lay down in the cool dirt and purred like a cat, he was so happy. They both stretched out in the dirt till the mosquitoes attacked them, then they hid under the sunflowers where Mr. Rumble rolled over so Mr. Bumble could lick the bites on his back.

Then they traded places and the hippo gave his master a lick, curling him up in the long pink carpet till he disappeared. When Mr. Bumble rolled back out, he felt as long and sleek as a dachshund.

Everything Mr. Bumble had always wanted to do was twice as much fun with his pet, and no one could tell him not to do it. He wondered how he had ever enjoyed his life before he got his pet hippo.

Now he finally understood why he made his mistress Jane so happy, too. Sometimes he'd wondered why just bumbling along on the end of a leash and letting himself be hugged and kissed could please her so much. But now that he had someone to take out for a walk, someone he wanted to touch and lick for no reason at all—now he knew just how she felt.

If only she could see his own pet! Then she'd know he understood! But he could only bring Mr. Rumble out when he was sleeping, so he could never show his hippo to his mistress Jane.

❋ ❋ ❋

One sunny Sunday the next spring, Mr. Bumble took a long afternoon walk with his mistress Jane and Mr. Grumble. It was such a beautiful day even Mr. Grumble couldn't find anything to grumble about, and his mistress Jane wasn't in a hurry, and more than once she let Mr. Bumble sniff as long as he wanted before they moved on.

That night, when it was time to go to sleep, Mr. Bumble jumped up on the bed for his biscuits. They always tasted so good he couldn't help drooling a little, waiting to take the first bite. His mistress Jane told him to sit, then she gave him three very small biscuits. Plus one more made four, "Because we had such a long walk today, Mr. Bumble."

After he ate his four tiny biscuits, Mr. Bumble lay down and was almost asleep when Mr. Grumble got into bed and said, "It was such a beautiful day, I hardly knew how to enjoy it!"

"Shhh!" Jane said to him. "Go to sleep, now. Didn't we have a wonderful time walking Mr. Bumble? Is there anything that could have been better?"

"We did have a wonderful time," Mr. Grumble agreed, "but it's already over, which shows there's always something wrong if you just think about it."

He slid his feet down under Mr. Bumble, who at the moment had to agree that Mr. Grumble was right, and grumbled himself as he got up and found the one place not filled with long legs jutting into his space at the end of the bed. He flopped down with a loud sigh and closed his eyes. As he settled himself among the blanketed feet, he felt the soft spring breeze blow in through the windows and heard the peepers peeping way over in the swamp by Werner's Pond.

But when he had slipped down into the strange and wonderful world of sleep where nothing weighed anything, not even a hippo, he could still feel the breeze and hear the peepers, and he knew tonight was so special he was going to have to take Mr. Rumble out for a walk. They had never gone out at night before but the hippo was right there, waiting for Mr. Bumble to fasten the leash around his thick gray neck, as eager to go out for a walk as his master, who told him that on this special spring night they were going to go many places, some they had never been to before.

They started up the road through the village and Mr. Rumble was so enthralled by the night he stopped to look up at the sky. With his huge gray and pink snout, he pointed out stars—Arcturus and Regulus, Polaris and Vega. "There's Cassiopeia, too. Look how bright it is!" he exclaimed.

The hippo seemed to know the names of lots of dots of light.

"There's the Big Nipper," said Mr. Bumble, not to be left out. It was the only constellation he knew. He remembered his mistress Jane pointing it out, though he wasn't quite sure he was pointing to the same one.

"It's the Big *Dipper*," Mr. Rumble sniffed, as if any terrier should know that.

"Let's go find a cabbage," said Mr. Bumble, changing the subject.

They continued up the road past all the sleeping houses and silent, invisible dogs, everything so quiet it was as if the small terrier and the large hippo were the only ones left in the village. The House of Many Woofs was so perfectly still there might have been no one inside, not even a mouse or a goldfish.

"We've got the whole world to ourselves," said Mr. Bumble as they walked through the village.

He spoke very softly because the breeze was hushing everything to be quiet.

"There's no one else out on this beautiful night—no one but us," he whispered to the hippo.

They were approaching the church when Mr. Bumble felt a tug on the leash.

"Look!" said Mr. Rumble. "There's someone coming!"

And there was.

Someone was walking down the road toward them.

She had long golden-red hair and two long legs, and looked so much like his mistress Jane that Mr. Bumble would have sworn on a whole box of biscuits that's who it was.

Except she didn't have her dog.

And she was crying.

"Oh, I've lost him, I've lost him!" she wailed as Mr. Bumble and the hippo came closer. "Where can he be? I can't live without him!"

"Who?" said Mr. Bumble, as he hurried up to see what was wrong.

She stopped in the middle of the road to see who had answered her cry. Through her tears, she saw what looked like a bumblebee leading a big gray school bus.

"My dog!" she exclaimed. "The back door blew open in the breeze and he took himself out for a walk! I'm just sure he'll run into Commander Bark's chows or have his neck broken by Tyrannosaurus Taurus!"

"I know just how you feel," said Mr. Bumble. "I'd feel awful if anything happened to my pet."

He reached up to give Mr. Rumble a lick on the side of his nose, but Mr. Rumble was turning away to root under a tree for a cabbage.

"Will you help me look for my dog?" said the lady with the golden-red hair. "Please!"

"Yes, of course. What does he look like?" asked Mr. Bumble, who wished he could do something to make her stop crying.

The lady looked down at him.

"He looks just like *you*!" she almost shouted, and sat down on the grass in a heap.

She started weeping so terribly Mr. Bumble couldn't stand it. He jumped up in her lap and began licking her face, then suddenly felt himself swept up in her arms.

"Oh, that's just what *my* dog used to do!" she cried, hugging and squeezing Mr. Bumble close to her chest. "If only you really *were* my own dog!"

"But I am!" said Mr. Bumble.

He couldn't help it. The truth had popped out before he could stop himself. Because as soon as he licked her face and tasted her tears, he knew that the lady with the golden-red hair was his mistress Jane.

"But you can't be!" she cried, squeezing him even harder. "You're just exactly like him, and I wish you were him more than anything—but my dog doesn't have a hippo!"

"A hippo?" said Mr. Bumble. It took him a moment to remember that's what his pet really was, because to him Mr. Rumble was Mr. Rumble, his pet and companion.

"Yes! Look!" she exclaimed, "I can see him myself!"

She pointed at Mr. Rumble, who had sat down and rolled over to get a better look at the stars.

"He's right there on the end of the leash!"

Mr. Bumble looked at his hippo gazing up at the starry sky and then back at his mistress Jane. Her eyes were starting to fill with tears once again.

"You mean, if I didn't have a hippo," said Mr. Bumble, trying to understand, "I'd be your very own dog?"

"Oh, I'm sure you would be," she said, squeezing him tightly again, "because it's really the only thing wrong with you!"

Mr. Bumble didn't think there was anything wrong with him at all, unless it was having such very short legs—which was hardly the same as having a hippo—but it wasn't something he could argue about because now a fresh tear had rolled down her cheek.

He licked it and made up his mind.

"Yes," Mr. Bumble conceded, "he is a hippo, but he's not exactly mine. It's hard to explain because I don't really know where he came from. But sometimes we go out for a walk together. And tonight was so beautiful . . ." Mr. Bumble hesitated; then he said, ". . . I was taking him outside the village to set him free."

"Set him free?" said his mistress Jane, looking confused.

"So I can go home with you," said Mr. Bumble.

"Really?" she said. "Would you do that for me?"

Mr. Bumble paused and looked at his hippo again. He almost felt a tear in his own eyes, then he turned and saw the joy on his mistress Jane's face.

"Yes," he said. "Yes, I would. I think Mr. Rumble is unhappy only coming out when I'm asleep, so I've decided to let him go."

"Let's hurry! Let's go!" his mistress Jane said, jumping up. "Then we'll go home and I'll give you a biscuit and we'll curl up in bed!"

They walked back through the village and turned down toward Werner's Pond and the swamp. As they walked along, Mr. Bumble felt Mr. Rumble on the end of the leash and, in spite of himself, one big tear leaked out of each of his eyes. But he didn't want his mistress Jane to know how sad he was to lose his pet hippo, so he just said, "It's a beautiful night, isn't it?"

"I hadn't noticed till now," his mistress Jane said, "but it really is. I think it's the most beautiful night I've ever seen."

When they got to the swamp, it suddenly became very quiet. The peepers all stopped peeping to hear what would happen next.

Mr. Bumble gave his hippo a last lick on his nose and unhooked the leash. Mr. Rumble didn't say goodbye, he just rumbled off into the swamp, splashing and disturbing the peepers, who had to dive deep into the mud so they wouldn't get squashed.

Watching his hippo splash off through the swamp, Mr. Bumble forgave Mr. Rumble for not looking back. A hippo has a very short memory, he said to himself, except maybe for stars.

Then Mr. Bumble remembered all the wonderful walks they had taken together, and the way all the dogs respected a dog who had his own pet, and for a moment he wished he hadn't let his hippo go. Then he looked up and saw his mistress Jane's face.

She was crying again, but this time it was because she was so happy. She bent down and put the hippo's leash around Mr. Bumble's neck.

"I'm sorry," she said, "but we wouldn't want to run into Commander Bark's chows or Tyrannosaurus Taurus in case the breeze blew one of their doors open, too."

They walked back through the village under the stars, past all the sleeping houses and down the road toward home.

When Mr. Bumble paused briefly to sniff the spot in the road where he and his hippo had stopped to look at the starry sky, he heard his mistress Jane exclaim:

"Oh, look! There's the Big Nipper!"

"Dipper," Mr. Bumble heard someone say in a voice so deep it rumbled under his paws.

But the sound was smothered by the finches singing way up in the trees, waiting to flock down to the feeders for breakfast, and he realized he was awake.

It was another beautiful day. The room was full of bright sunlight, his mistress Jane was asleep, and Mr. Grumble was just waking up.

"Look what time it is!" he said, grabbing his watch by the side of the bed. "I'll never get anything done!"

He jumped out of bed with a sigh, and the falling blankets almost covered Mr. Bumble where he lay in his spot by his mistress Jane's feet.

She sat up and opened her eyes, rubbing them as if she'd been crying.

"Oh, I had the most frightening dream!" she said. "I dreamt I lost Mr. Bumble and I couldn't find him anywhere. I was sure he was gone forever! Then I found him just walking along by himself, as if nothing in the world was wrong!"

Yes, thought Mr. Bumble, and who else did you see? Who else was with Mr. Bumble?

"Why did you do that?" she said, looking at him angrily. "Why did you take yourself out for a walk and scare me like that?"

She scooped him up in her arms and hugged him and kissed him.

"Don't you know how sad I'd be if anything happened to you?"

Yes, I know, Mr. Bumble said to himself, licking her face.

He had seen for himself just how sad she would be, and now he didn't mind if she squeezed him too hard because he also knew that, even if his mistress Jane's memory wasn't much better than a hippo's, it was his job to be hugged and kissed, and to lick her face and make her happy, and to bumble along on the end of her leash.

2. Mr Bumble Takes a Ride

*O*h, Mr. Bumble, I love you so much!" his mistress Jane cried as she squeezed him so hard his ribs pinched together.

It was at least a year later, or maybe two, or even three, and Mr. Bumble was in a familiar place—his mistress Jane's arms—when she told him she was going to leave him alone in the house for a while.

She put him down on the floor and held out a dog biscuit which he took in his teeth, carefully avoiding the ends of her fingers.

"I'll be back soon," she said as she opened the front door, "and if anyone comes and knocks on the door and scares you while I'm gone, please try not to make a mark on the floor."

She closed the door behind her and Mr. Bumble jumped up on the couch to watch her walk down the road. He never meant to make a mark on the floor with his water, and he only did it when someone made a great racket and he couldn't get out to chase them away.

When his mistress Jane disappeared beyond the last tree, he jumped off the couch—with the biscuit still in his mouth—and ran upstairs, where he jumped up on the bed and looked out the window. Now he could see past the last tree to . . . another tree, but she was already gone. He stood for a moment with his forepaws up on the headboard of the bed and tried to sniff the world through the pane of glass. But he couldn't. There was a goldfinch in the ash tree outside the window, right there in the front yard, free to hop from branch to branch or fly away if he wanted, but Mr. Bumble was shut inside the house. He hopped down from the head-board, ate the biscuit in three bites, turned around twice, and lay down with a sigh.

As he closed his eyes to take a nap, he thought of Mr. Rumble, his pet hippo, and wished he still had him. Once, whenever Mr. Bumble lay down for a nap, he knew the hippo would be there waiting to be taken out for a ramble or an adventure. But that was before the starry night one spring when he let Mr. Rumble go in the swamp. When he woke up the next morning, he realized he didn't have his pet any-more. Now, starting to doze, he remembered the great gray body, the odd tiny ears, and the huge pink cavern guarded by white pillars that rose up taller than Mr. Bumble himself when the hippo yawned. Where had he gone when he splashed away in the swamp? How had he suddenly appeared the first time? Mr. Bumble wished he could see the hippo again just to find out.

The bright, sunny world on the other side of his closed eyelids became a haze, and as he dozed he saw a landscape that looked like the swamp around Werner's Pond. He heard the singing and croaking peepers, and saw them leaping into the sky over a hippo—over tens and hundreds and thousands of hippos—and he felt one big tear leaking out of each eye when all the hippos ran away through the swamp—
Thump!
—under a sky sprinkled with cabbages, cabbages that twinkled like stars—
Thump!
—and flying hippos chased starry cabbages—
THUMP!
—and flying cabbages chased starry hippos—
THUM-UMMP!
—and a small golden-red dog was flying himself, through the stars and cabbages and dog biscuits too, all flying, flying downstairs, barking and snarling to chase away whatever monster was making the terrific thumping against the front door!

As Mr. Bumble slid down the last five steps on his belly, he knew nothing could stop him—he was going to have to make a mark on the floor if he couldn't drive this tremendous thumping away.

But when he flopped at the bottom of the stairs, the front door suddenly flew wide open—and a cabbage rolled in.

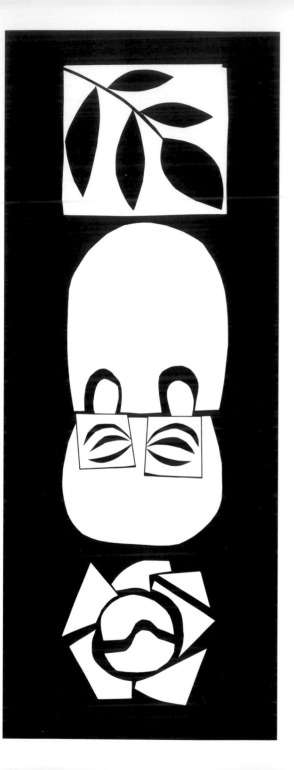

Mr. Bumble scrambled up, his paws slipping on the slick floor, ran to the cabbage and sniffed it. As he lifted his leg to mark the cabbage, he looked up and saw something outside in the front yard—something that *filled* the front yard.

Standing under the ash tree with a cabbage poised in its mouth was a hippopotamus.

When he saw Mr. Bumble, the hippo dropped the cabbage and said with annoyance, "Didn't you hear me? I thought I was going to have to use all my cabbages to knock down the door!"

"Mister Rumble!" Mr. Bumble exclaimed.

In reply, the hippo deftly kicked the cabbage he'd just dropped. It shot forward, bounced off the front step, and ricocheted high in the air. A moment later, it dropped from the sky and disappeared down Mr. Rumble's throat with a gulp.

"You almost *did* knock it down," said Mr. Bumble, rather annoyed himself, "and you made such a racket you made me have an accident on the floor!"

"Come on," said the hippo, ignoring the scolding, "let's go for a walk."

"A walk?" Mr. Bumble was confused. That starry night in the swamp when Mr. Rumble splashed away through the peepers, he hadn't said goodbye—or looked back even once at his master standing by the road. Now Mr. Rumble had come back by himself.

Mr. Bumble went out on the front steps into the sunlight to make sure this really was the same hippo, and before he could stop himself, he asked, "Did you miss me?"

"I want to show you something," said the hippo, ignoring the question.

"What is it? Don't tell me you have a pet now, too!"

"A pet? No, pets are a nuisance."

"A nuisance?" Mr. Bumble had never thought his pet was a nuisance and he certainly didn't think of himself as a nuisance to his mistress Jane. He hoped she didn't think he was either.

"Are you coming?" said the hippo.

"What do you want to show me?" said Mr. Bumble.

"I can't tell you—it's a surprise. You'll have to sniff it for yourself," he said, thrusting his own massive snout in the air.

Mr. Bumble hesitated. "Okay, I'll come with you." Then he added, "Wait a minute while I get the leash."

"No," said the hippo, "you don't need a leash. I won't run away, not unless you want me to. I'd rather you think of me as a friend instead of a pet."

"A friend?"

"Yes. If you don't mind."

"What kind of friend?" Mr. Bumble wasn't sure what this new relationship meant.

"A good one. One you can trust. Come on!"

"Oh, I trust you," said Mr. Bumble, not sure why he should or even if he really did.

Mr. Rumble was already rumbling down the road.

Without thinking about what he was doing, Mr. Bumble jumped off the front steps and bumbled down the road after him.

For someone so large, the hippo could move very fast without even running, and the small, golden-red dog was already far behind by the time he ran past the House of Many Woofs. He followed the great gray rump and the tree-trunk legs on through the village, past the church, then down the road, watching the odd little tail that twitched back and forth. Now they were out of the village but Mr. Bumble still hadn't caught up; in fact he was falling even further behind and began to wonder if the hippo was teasing him. It was too warm a day to be running so hard and so fast, and he was about to give up and turn back when he looked up and saw Mr. Rumble standing in the middle of the road up ahead, waiting for him.

"I'm sorry," he said as Mr. Bumble caught up. "I forgot you're so small."

"Well, that's strange," Mr. Bumble said, panting so hard his tongue almost touched the ground, "because I never forget you're so large."

"That's something I never give any thought to at all," said the hippo.

"If you met an elephant or a brontosaurus, you might notice size does make a difference," said the dog.

"Well, we're never going to get there if I have to keep waiting for you," said Mr. Rumble.

"Then you'd better go on by yourself," said Mr. Bumble, "because it's a very hot day and I can't take off this fur coat."

"But I want to show you a surprise—and it's not a surprise if I go by myself to see something I've already seen," said Mr. Rumble.

"I want to see it," said Mr. Bumble, "but this wouldn't be the first time I was disappointed."

Mr. Rumble looked up at the clear blue sky for a moment, then he said, "I have an idea. You can ride on my back."

"On your back? That's a wonderful idea!" Mr. Bumble looked up at Mr. Rumble's bulging gray side looming above him like a mountain. "But how could I ever get up there?"

Mr. Rumble squinted his great bulbous eyes as he sized up the very small dog. "Can you jump up on my nose?"

The hippo bent his forelegs and lowered his snout to the ground.

Mr. Bumble looked at the broad gray and pink nose and decided it really wasn't much higher than the couch or the bed.

"I can try," he said.

He braced himself, jumped as high as he could, and landed right between the nostrils, where he was tickled by some whiskers he'd never noticed before. He scrambled up the long slope of the snout, and as he ran between Mr. Rumble's eyes he saw them cross. Then up toward the top of the brow between the ears, where it was so steep that his paws started slipping on the rough hide and he felt himself sliding back down.

"Lift your head, Mr. Rumble, lift up your head!" he shouted.

The head rose up like an elevator, the steep hill became a gentle slope, and Mr. Bumble ran up over the dome to the top of the shoulders, where he saw an expanse as broad as a sidewalk.

What a view—he was on top of the world! Instead of looking up at everything the way he'd done his whole life, now he was looking down. There was the top of a mailbox, the roof of a car, and over the stone wall he could see a field full of flowers. The ground was so far below it made him dizzy.

"Are you all right up there?" called the hippo, his voice sounding very far away.

"I feel like I'm going to fall off, it's so high!" Mr. Bumble called back.

"Don't shout!" Mr. Rumble winced. "My ear is right in front of you."

Mr. Bumble looked at the funnel-shaped pink and gray ear; it wasn't even as tall as he was. "I'm sorry," he said into it quietly, then started investigating his new perch.

"Please settle down," he heard the distant voice say. "You're making me nervous with all that pacing about."

"I'm not pacing," said Mr. Bumble. "There isn't *that* much room."

"Well, you're doing something," said the hippo, "and I don't like it."

"I'm looking around. It's exciting up here!"

Indeed, Mr. Bumble was so excited being up at this height that he had run down the hippo's back to peer over his rump, then back up to his shoulders to the spot high above his front legs. Then he tried to find a firm spot for his paws, so he wouldn't fall off as soon as they started moving.

"Maybe this isn't such a good idea," Mr. Bumble said. "I think I'll come back down."

"Just try it," said the hippo. "I'll go slowly at first. Once you get used to it, I bet you'll never want to come down."

They started off. At first Mr. Bumble was sure he'd been right. The huge gray back rolled from side to side like a barrel and with each step he was sure he was about to slide off. But after just a short distance he began to get used to the rhythm, and by the time they came down the hill past Pete and Henry's Cafe, he felt almost as much at ease as he was when he stood on the gold couch at home.

When they crossed the river he looked over the side of the hippo to the bridge far below, then way down over the bridge to the water tumbling over the rocks. He felt so high above the earth he thought he must be flying and wondered if this was the surprise Mr. Rumble wanted to show him.

They turned up the road and cruised past a German shepherd who jumped on top of his doghouse, both frightened and curious at the sight of a terrier riding through the countryside on a hippo. They passed a cow by a fence and Mr. Bumble could see right over its head. He could see into the windows of houses and over the tops of the cars on the expressway . . . .

Where were they?

They seemed to be soaring along, and he'd never seen any of this countryside before except from the car. How had they come so far in such a short time? He was suddenly scared. What if he fell off and Mr. Rumble didn't even notice? How would he ever get home again?

"Mr. Rumble!" he shouted. "Where are we? Where are we going?"

"I told you, you don't have to *shout*," shouted the hippo. "Can't you see my ear—both of them—right there in front of you?"

"Is this the surprise?" Mr. Bumble said into one of the odd little ears which, because they were soaring so fast, lay almost flat in the wind.

"Just be patient. You'll see," said Mr. Rumble. "You're almost as impatient as your mistress Jane!"

As impatient as her? He hoped not! How did Mr. Rumble know what she was like, anyway? It was amazing. *Everything* was amazing . . . .

Whoaaaaa!

They took a sharp turn and Mr. Bumble bent his knees and flattened himself against the hippo's back so he wouldn't fly off.

Now they were in the city, weaving through traffic like a taxi, dodging trucks and buses, sideswiping a policeman so closely they brushed the end of his nose. They leaped over a hole in the street where men in steel hats were digging with air hammers, turned another corner, and suddenly Mr. Bumble smelled something familiar. He looked up, and there was the red brick building where his mistress Jane once had her studio and had taken him with her to work every day. Up in the window he saw the Cat Who Wouldn't Be Sniffed!

They glided on, downhill and up, and then down again. A moment later they were gliding down the very street Mr. Bumble used to live on—and there was the Galloping Galoot himself! Sniffing the sudden approach of Mr. Bumble, the Galoot's mouth opened, but when he saw the enormous creature the golden-red dog was mounted on, the woof caught in his throat, his eyes rolled up in his head, and his tongue hung over his teeth like a flag of surrender.

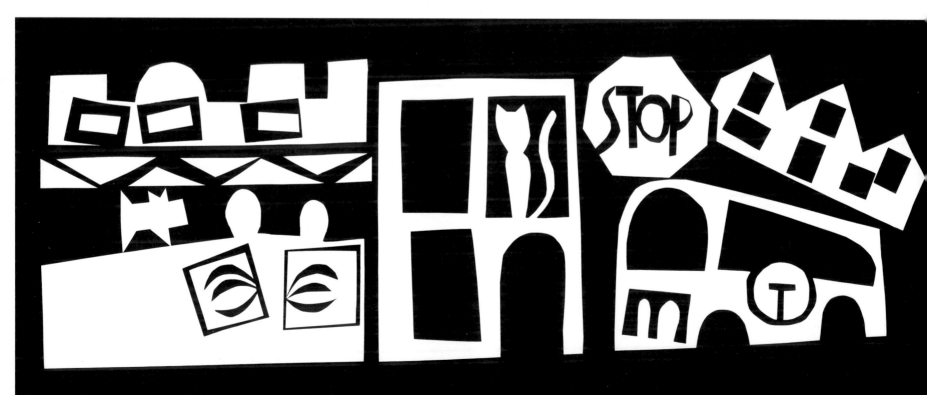

"What a *terrific* surprise!" Mr. Bumble roared as he launched a volley of fierce barks at the limp Galoot.

They swerved around the corner and there was Attila the Pit Bull! The bronze-plated cur jumped out of their way so fast he almost yanked the Smoking Woman holding his leash into the bushes.

Mr. Bumble hurled his most ferocious snarl at the quaking Attila, remembering the time he attacked Laundromat Derek for no reason at all, except that Derek was old and Attila was crazy.

"What a *glorious* surprise!" Mr. Bumble shouted. "Take me around the block again!"

His final triumphant snarl trailed down the street behind them.

At the corner, Mr. Rumble stopped short and Mr. Bumble almost slid down his nose.

"This is *not* your surprise," said Mr. Rumble, sounding very annoyed, "and I'm disappointed you'd think only about showing off and getting revenge when you have a chance to come back to where you came from. I really would have thought better of you than that."

"I'd like to think better of myself than that too," said Mr. Bumble, "but if you'd spent your whole life having to look up to a fire hydrant instead of being as big as a school bus, you might want a little revenge too!"

Mr. Rumble twisted his head around to look up at the small dog perched high on his back. "Well, maybe so," he conceded, "but that still doesn't make it dignified, and now I almost feel like taking you home without showing you the surprise."

"I've already had a wonderful surprise, just riding on your back, and I thank you for that," said Mr. Bumble, "but do you know what the Galloping Galoot or Attila the Pit Bull would have done to me if they'd ever caught me alone on the street?"

"Let's just forget it," said Mr. Rumble, "and agree that there are some things hippos and terriers can't see the same way."

"That should be as obvious as the difference in our sizes," said Mr. Bumble, who didn't mean to offend Mr. Rumble but couldn't help feeling misunderstood.

"But we should also agree," continued the hippo, "that as long as we're together you don't have to bark and snarl at other dogs, no matter how they might have treated you before we were friends."

"Friends." He had said it again. At first Mr. Rumble had been his pet. Now they were friends. That meant they were equals, didn't it? What was next? Was the hippo going to put a collar around his neck and make Mr. Bumble *his* pet? Was that the surprise?

"You didn't answer me," said the hippo, once again twisting his head around to look up at his passenger.

"Okay," said Mr. Bumble, "I won't start any trouble, and if someone else does then you can finish it."

"Fine," said Mr. Rumble, and started off again.

"But," said Mr. Bumble into the small gray funnel-shaped ear.

The hippo stopped.

"Just because you're as big as a school bus and I have to look up to a fire hydrant doesn't mean I can let you tell me what to do."

"Tell you what to do?" echoed Mr. Rumble. "I certainly know better than to try to do that. Not only would you resent it—and rightly so—it would also be *most* undignified for me to take advantage of you because of my greater size. When it comes to rights and respect, a terrier is just as great as a hippo, or even an elephant or a brontosaurus."

"That's just what I think," said Mr. Bumble, "and it's the reason I sometimes have to make so much noise. There are so many Galoots and Attilas of various kinds who don't have your high standard of respect for an individual's dignity."

"I appreciate the compliment," said Mr. Rumble. "Now, do you want to go home, or shall we go find the surprise?"

Mr. Bumble hesitated, then leaned forward and whispered into the comically small ear that had twisted around to hear his answer: "Is a hippo bigger than a terrier?"

He heard a snort, and a deep chuckle vibrated under his paws in the depths of the great gray barrel he was mounted on.

It was a neighborhood he had only passed through once or twice with his mistress Jane and Mr. Grumble on long Sunday walks. The street was wide, with tall leafy maples arching over houses so big they looked as if even a hippo could live in one. For a moment, Mr. Bumble wondered if that was the surprise, to see where Mr. Rumble lived. Maybe he had a house with its own river to loll in while servants rolled cabbages to him and visitors were served their choice of meat.

They stopped in front of a double iron gate set in a high, bristly hedge. The hippo nudged the gate with his nose, it swung open wide, and they walked down a driveway toward a grand brick house, big enough for a family of hippos. But instead of going to the front door, they went around the house to the back where a broad yard was surrounded by a wrought iron fence. Mr. Rumble continued up to the fence, which had no gate but was attached to the back of the house, and stopped.

"Look!" said Mr. Rumble.

"What?" said Mr. Bumble.

Perched on the hippo's back, Mr. Bumble was high enough to see over the closely spaced metal pickets, but all he could see was a vast green lawn, so perfectly groomed it looked like a rug instead of grass. There was a flower garden at one end with a birdbath in the middle, several dogwoods around the yard, and a border of rose bushes with bright red blooms climbing the fence all the way around. At the far end was a copper beech with a gray trunk as thick as a hippo's neck. The scene was so lovely it didn't look real, but if this was Mr. Rumble's surprise, it was a bit disappointing.

"It's a very beautiful yard," said Mr. Bumble politely.

"Is that all you can see?" said Mr. Rumble. "What's wrong with your eyes? What's wrong with your *nose*?"

"My nose? Nothing is wrong with—"

"Yip!" someone cried.

Yip? Mr. Bumble sniffed the air and smelled something—something rare, very rare, and intoxicating.

"Yip yip yip!"

"Look down, Mr. Bumble," the hippo suggested, "look *way* down."

Mr. Bumble leaned over the great gray brow and looked down the long snout, and there by the bottom edge of the fence, just a few inches from the end of Mr. Rumble's nose, was a small—a very, *very* small—silver-black dog. Mr. Rumble pressed his nose against the fence and the very small silver-black dog reached through the bars to give him a thousand quick licks in greeting.

"I've brought you a surprise," Mr. Rumble said through the fence. Then he stepped back and spoke to the golden-red dog standing high up on his brow, who was now staring in wonder at the very small dog on the other side of the fence.

"Mr. Bumble, don't you want to come down?"

Even from the great height of the hippo's head, Mr. Bumble could tell that the very small dog, whose delicate nose he could see through the bars of the fence, was a Miss, not a Mister, and a very attractive one too. Yet, Mr. Bumble hesitated. In spite of his trim figure and lively spirit, he was no longer a young pup. He was an older gent now, and it had been some time since he had allowed himself to indulge in romantic fantasies. It was undignified, and besides, he had never had a real lady friend in his whole life, and it embarrassed him so much to admit this that he had begun pretending he had never wanted one anyway.

"Ohhh . . ." he heard someone whispering, ". . . is that who you were telling me about?"

Mr. Bumble peeked around the small gray funnel-shaped ear he was hiding behind, and as he did, he saw a pair of dark eyes looking up at him through the fence. He jumped back and almost rolled right off Mr. Rumble.

"Yes, that's him," said Mr. Rumble, "and I don't know why he's so shy. You should have seen him just a minute ago when he saw the Galloping Galoot!"

Hearing the name of his nemesis, Mr. Bumble stood back up, squared his small but sturdy conformation, and marched over the hippo's brow. He continued down the long length of the nose and stopped at the end with his paws between the two great hollow pink nostrils.

"How do you do?" he said with great dignity.

Two astonished, tiny dark eyes gazed at him through the space in the fence.

"My name is Mister Bumble and I'm pleased to meet you," he finished.

"How do you do," returned the very small silver-black dog, whose coat was so long and lustrous it reached all the way down to the ground. "I'm pleased to meet you too. My name is Mrs. Troughear's Little Dot of Darlington."

"Mrs. Truffle's Little Bit of . . . ? " Mr. Bumble mumbled, and in his nervousness forgot the rest.

"They call me Dottie," she said, nodding her silver and ebony head toward the huge brick house.

"I call her Miss Tumble," the hippo said out of the side of his mouth. He gave a chuckle which the small dog on his nose could feel vibrating under his paws.

"Miss Tumble?" Mr. Bumble repeated.

"Miss . . . *Tumble*!" Mr. Rumble repeated again with a fresh snort of amusement, so strong that it blew Mr. Bumble off the end of his nose. He landed upside-down, by the edge of the fence right in front of her.

"Oh! Are you hurt?" cried Miss Tumble.

"I'm fine, thank you," Mr. Bumble said, as he scrambled up quickly and shook himself off.

"I'm sorry," Mr. Rumble apologized. "Here, jump back up on my nose and I'll lift you over the fence. If Miss Tumble doesn't mind."

"Not at all," she said. "I'd love some civilized company."

Mr. Bumble braced himself, jumped, and scrambled up the hippo's nose. It wasn't as easy with someone watching, and he had to put one paw in Mr. Rumble's nostril to pull himself up.

"Ow!" the hippo exclaimed, giving a shudder that shook the ground and almost threw Mr. Bumble off again.

"Sorry," Mr. Bumble said, as he ran up the long snout, between the eyes, and up over the brow to his perch just behind the funnel-shaped ears.

The huge head rose like a crane and this time Mr. Bumble wasn't dizzy at all, but stood tall and proud on his perch. The hippo stretched his neck over the fence, which wasn't nearly as high as it was long, then leaned his head down as far as he could.

"Jump!" said Mr. Rumble.

"Jump!" said Miss Tumble.

Mr. Bumble jumped and landed almost gracefully on the green lawn. It was so thick and soft he sank up to his knees in the grass.

"Oh! Are you all right?" Miss Tumble yelped with sympathy.

"Am I all right?" Mr. Bumble repeated as he glanced back at the huge gray nose just above him.

The nose gave a soft snort and, as the great head slowly swung back over the fence, Mr. Rumble murmured, "Is a hippo bigger than a terrier?"

Mr. Bumble had landed in heaven. The deep lawn, bordered with roses and dotted with dogwoods (his favorite tree) and set off by the copper beech with a trunk as thick as a hippo's neck, must be the place terriers go who have tamed their fierce tempers and behaved with dignity. It was shot through with sunlight and dappled with shade, and at the center was the very small silver-black Little Dot of Darlington. As she strolled by his side through the soft grass, her shimmering coat trailed through the blades, and Miss Tumble told the story of how she had come to live here.

"I was born in the kennel of a famous breeder of Yorkshire terriers outside New York and brought here by my master, who's a Full Professor of Something Very Important at a World Famous University," she said. "He's written many thick books and travels all over the world, and his hobby is showing dogs."

"Showing dogs what?" asked Mr. Bumble, who was very fond of his own master and loved his mistress Jane dearly, but they had never shown him anything useful at all, although it was true they weren't even half-full professors of anything, important or not.

"No, no," Miss Tumble explained, "he shows dogs to people."

"Don't the people notice the dogs by themselves?" asked Mr. Bumble, who felt that if people weren't interested in him, he wouldn't bother to sniff them either.

"You don't understand," said Miss Tumble, sounding almost annoyed. She described how she rode in a cage in the back of a car and sometimes even flew in a big silver tube across the whole country to go to halls and malls and auditoriums where dogs of every kind in the world were brushed and combed and powdered and then ran around in rings in front of men in suits and women wearing corsages who judged which dog was best and awarded them ribbons and trophies.

"They should let the dogs decide which dog is best," said Mr. Bumble, "and if the judges want to judge something, they could judge the owners and give them the ribbons and trophies. I'd rather win a nice piece of meat and maybe go for a walk, myself."

"Oh, but if you win enough ribbons and trophies, they make a fuss over you as if you were royalty," said Miss Tumble. "I've been Best of Breed many times and once I was even Best of Show. I'm a champion."

"You certainly look like one to me," said Mr. Bumble, "and I'm an excellent judge of dogs. Especially terriers."

"Oh, excuse me," she said quickly. "I didn't mean to boast. That's very bad manners."

"I don't mind," he said. "I'm sure you'd win Best of Show every time if the dogs were doing the judging."

"Well, I'm retired now, anyway," she said with a sigh.

"Retired? You can't be—you look so young!" said Mr. Bumble.

"We quit the ring rather early. Besides . . . I'm probably not quite as young as I look," she confessed.

"Neither am I," said Mr. Bumble. "At least that's what my mistress Jane always tells people."

They had stopped under the beech tree and as Miss Tumble spoke she turned away shyly. With her movement, a delicate whiff of her feminine dogness wafted on the light breeze into Mr. Bumble's cool wet nose, and he suddenly felt as young as he looked.

"It's so beautiful here where you live," he sighed as a strange, exciting sensation surged through him.

"Yes, it is," she replied. "But sometimes I feel sort of lonely . . . and even bored. My master doesn't like me to play with anyone, even now that I'm retired, because I might get dirty and soil my coat."

"I spend most of my time alone, too," said Mr. Bumble. "My mistress Jane keeps me away from other dogs so I won't bite them—before they bite me," he added quickly. "But I only bite male dogs, and I only bite them if they're bigger than me. I'd never pick on anyone my own size."

"That's very admirable," said Miss Tumble. "What's your mistress like? Is she good to you? Are you happy living with her?"

"Oh, yes. Mostly," he said. "Although it's true that, as well as she treats me, sometimes I get lonely too . . . and even a little bored. That's why I got my hippo. At first he was my pet, but now . . . " he glanced around the yard but didn't see Mr. Rumble's great gray back anywhere over the fence, " . . . now, he's more like a friend."

"He must be a very good friend, because he told me how much he liked you," said Miss Tumble. Then, as if she'd just had an idea, she exclaimed, "If you're lonely too, maybe you and Mr. Rumble could come and live here!"

"With you?" said Mr. Bumble incredulously.

"Oh, well, I didn't mean . . . " Miss Tumble's black nose turned mauve with embarrassment and she dropped her eyes.

Mr. Bumble was so touched by her modesty that without thinking he suddenly leaned toward her and gave her a tiny nip on the ear.

Miss Tumble jumped back and cried, "Mis-ter Bum-ble!" Her dark eyes blazed at him in the sunlight.

Then she nipped him back and scampered off through the grass.

He chased after her, zigging and zagging right behind, and just as he caught up to her, she stopped, turned, leaped in the air and tumbled right over him. Then she raced off in the other direction, yipping with joy.

Yapping with surprise, Mr. Bumble chased her again. She led him around the dogwoods in figure eights until he was panting for air, then dashed off and disappeared behind the copper beech. When he almost caught her coming around the thick-as-a-hippo's-neck trunk, she leaped in the air and tumbled over him again. Then she ran away yipping in triumph.

The small golden-red dog and the even smaller silver-black dog raced around and around the vast green yard, and when he nearly caught her again she darted under the rose bushes that covered the fence. As he chased her through the vines, he felt the thorns snagging his coat, pulling and tugging against him. Ahead, he saw Miss Tumble tumbling through the vines too—and suddenly he had caught up with her. She was trapped, tangled up in rose vines and shaggy with dirt, and she had one big red rose on top of her head like a crown.

"Oh, Mr. Bumble," she cried, still panting, "you finally caught me!"

"No, the rose vines caught you. Look, they caught me too!" He twisted and shook and finally yanked himself free. "Here, let me help you."

He bit the vines in his teeth and gently pulled them away from her coat, so they wouldn't pull out her hair. Then once again he sniffed her intoxicating dogness and, unable to help himself, he licked her nose.

Instead of objecting, she looked up into his eyes—and licked him back.

This was more than just a surprise; this was something he had never felt before in his life.

Carefully, deliberately, he licked her again.

Deliberately, carefully, she licked him again too.

Carefully, deliberately—

"Dottie! Dottie!"

"Uh-oh," she cried.

"Who's that?" said Mr. Bumble.

"That's my master calling me," she said quickly. "You'd better go!"

"Go?" Mr. Bumble looked around. The whole yard was fenced tight and the great gray mountain had disappeared.

"Will you come and see me again? Please!" she added.

"Yes, yes, I'll come back," he said, although at the moment he didn't even know how he was going to leave.

"Dottie, come here girl!" the deep voice shouted again.

Mr. Bumble gave her a quick lick to seal his promise to return.

"Soon!" she said and ran off toward the back of the house with the red rose still on her head, yipping loudly to distract her master.

"Here Dottie, here girl!"

The voice suddenly changed. "Dottie! What happened to you?"

It got louder, and angry:

"Hey—hey, you!"

Mr. Bumble knew right away it was shouting at him. As he ran out of the rose bushes and down the length of the yard, he not only heard but felt the footsteps pounding behind him on the grass. When he got to the end of the yard, he cut back sharply the other way and shot right under the long angry arm.

He sped around the edge of the yard by the border of rose bushes as fast as he could go, which was faster than the two long legs still pounding behind him. But there was no way out, there were no holes in the fence, and all he could do was dodge this way and that in the thick grass, avoiding the furious arms that kept grabbing for him.

"Come here, you mutt! Did you touch my precious? Did you get her all dirty?"

Mr. Bumble was so insulted he was terribly tempted to stop and bite Miss Tumble's master to show him he wasn't a mutt but a pedigreed Cairn terrier with all the papers to prove it. But he remembered Mr. Rumble's advice to remain dignified, and vowed not to be brought down to the Full Professor's level.

He led his pursuer around the copper beech, where one of the two long legs tripped on a root. He heard a WHUMP! and a cry of pain as he ran back down the lawn. Once again he'd gotten away, but he was still trapped in the yard, and looked back to see Miss Tumble's master limping toward him. He was ready to give up hope of escape and was choosing which leg to bite when he noticed a thick pink carpet draped over the fence and spread on the grass.

That hadn't been there before!

He ran to the carpet and leaped on it, hoping he could climb up it and over the fence. But as soon as his paws touched the pink rug, it started to move. It lifted him up off the ground and high in the air, above the two long angry arms that reached up to grab him. As it carried him over the fence, he saw two crater-sized quivering pink nostrils on the end of a massive gray snout, raised high to reveal the tall white toothy pillars in the great gaping mouth.

Mr. Rumble!

Mr. Bumble ran up the tongue, jumped on the nose, scrambled up over the brow, between the ears, and mounted up to his perch on the rough-hided broad gray shoulders . . . . And now they were bounding through the city, past trees and trucks and taxis and buildings, over bridges, through stoplights, around corners. On through the suburbs, gliding past station wagons and school buses, past a shopping mall, a car wash, a gas station, along the expressway and back out to the country.

This time, Mr. Bumble didn't even have to try to keep his balance or hold on tight with his paws. He felt as secure as a circus trick rider on a thundering horse or a jockey mounted on a thoroughbred, running around a racetrack. They flew on together, the great gray hippopotamus and the small golden-red terrier. As the wind whipped his ears and tugged at his fur and blew his tail out as straight as a pointer's, Mr. Bumble felt so thrilled and exhilarated that even if nothing else had happened, none of the other wonderful things—even if he hadn't met the enchanting Miss Tumble—just to soar and glide on Mr. Rumble's back with the whole silly world flying by was as big a surprise as a dog could ever want.

They were flying so fast that the countryside became a blur, a blur of spectacular shapes, then they passed through a shower of stars—stars and cabbages, cabbages and dog biscuits. The scent in the air was the intoxicating memory of Mrs. Troughear's Little Dot of Darlington, and the sound he heard was the sound of . . . of . . .

"Oh, Mr. Bumble! Mr. Bumble! You didn't even wake up when I came home! What's wrong? Are you all right?"

Am I all right? As he repeated the question to himself, he heard a deep voice rumble in reply, *Is a hippo bigger than a terrier?* and felt a chuckle vibrate somewhere under his paws.

His mistress Jane sat down on the bed beside him to give him a hug.

"You were so sound asleep you didn't even hear me, did you!" she said between kisses, then picked him up and carried him downstairs. "You used to wake up before I even opened the door. I guess you're just getting older, aren't you."

At the bottom of the stairs she stopped and her voice changed. "Oh, my, what happened here? I didn't see this before . . . ."

Mr. Bumble looked down expecting to see a cabbage by the front door but instead there was nothing; nothing but a small—a very small—puddle.

"Did something scare you? It's my fault, isn't it, leaving you alone all day in the house. That wasn't very considerate, was it."

She put him down on the floor and after she'd cleaned up the few drops—it was just a few drops, and he was sure he couldn't have left them there, anyway—she snapped the leash on his collar.

"I bet I know what you want. Let's go for a walk."

As she led him down the road past the trees, he bumbled along on the end of the leash and remembered the divine Miss Tumble in her heavenly yard, the way she ran and leaped on the thick green lawn in her shimmering silver-black coat, the scent of her dogness, the swooning sensation when he licked her nose, and then the last glimpse of her running across the yard with a red rose on her head like a crown. He remembered the Cat Who Wouldn't Be Sniffed up in the window, and his old neighborhood, and scaring the Galloping Galoot and Attila the Pit Bull. He also remembered, very briefly, Mr. Rumble's displeasure at his outburst. Then he remembered the moment he jumped on the long pink carpet, and the ride home on the hippo, a ride that could have gone on and on, all the way around the world . . . .

Suddenly Mr. Bumble realized that he'd forgotten to ask Mr. Rumble where he lived. Where had he gone after he splashed through the swamp, and where had he come from in the first place?

His mistress Jane led him up the road toward the House of Many Woofs. As they approached, the windows filled with furry faces, and the little house started woofing and bulging with the muffled voices of the ten dogs who lived there.

When Mr. Bumble heard the familiar sound, and smelled the familiar smells along the road, he was glad, in a way, to be home. And he decided that, if the hippo ever came back again, he would be sure to ask where he came from—and where he went when he was gone.

3. Mr Bumble Says Goodbye

*M*r. Bumble had grown old—very old—and although he couldn't understand why things should change just because he'd grown older and older, that's exactly what happened.

Everything seemed to be changing.

The biggest change was that he no longer liked to bumble along the way he used to.

When Mr. Grumble took him out in the morning, as soon as he'd taken care of his personal business, he was ready to turn right around and go home to eat breakfast. But Mr. Grumble always insisted, unless it was raining, that there were things Mr. Bumble should sniff, so they walked all the way up to the top of the hill before turning around.

When he bumbled down the road with his mistress Jane, he sometimes fell behind and the leash pulled the collar tight against his neck, not because he was sniffing something but because he was tired and wanted to go home. But she always wanted to go see Kate's sheep or walk out past Werner's Pond to the Lookout, or up to the milk barn and back down to the post office where the Lady with Letters and Gossip greeted his mistress Jane and said, "How's Mr. Bumble today?"

Tired, thought Mr. Bumble. *I'm really quite tired.*

"He's slowing down a bit," said his mistress Jane. "He'll be fifteen this winter, you know."

"Fifteen!" said the Lady with Letters and Gossip. "He doesn't look as if he's even half that old!"

"Oh, yes," said his mistress Jane. "He takes a long walk every day and that keeps him young. But each day we have together now is a bonus."

Mr. Bumble felt proud to hear the compliment but he wondered why he had to keep taking such long walks to all the same places. By now there was hardly anything that really needed to be sniffed. What would it matter if he just lay on the gold couch and spent a few more minutes asleep every day?

It had been quite a while since he'd seen Mr. Rumble. Sometimes he wondered if the hippo had grown older, too, and was no longer interested in going for walks either. Perhaps he was lying down somewhere, taking a nap and dreaming of cabbages. Or maybe the hippo had forgotten all about his small, golden-red friend and had someone else to take on trips now. But Mr. Bumble never thought about his old friend for long, because when he lay down for his nap in the morning, all he really wanted to do was sleep, and when Mr. Rumble didn't appear, Mr. Bumble was secretly glad. Or would have been glad, if he wasn't already asleep.

One warm day in the spring when all the snow had finally melted, Mr. Bumble curled up on the new bed his mistress Jane had gotten for him and put on the floor beside the table where she and Mr. Grumble ate their dinner. As he dozed off, he saw someone standing outside beside the garden. It took him a moment to realize who—or what—it was. Then the sight of his mountainous old friend filled Mr. Bumble with a very pleasing emotion, especially since Mr. Rumble looked equally happy to see him. But as pleasant as it was seeing his friend again,

Mr. Bumble didn't quite feel like going for a walk or even a ride, so instead he lay comfortably where he was, on the soft bed by the dining room table, and remembered the adventurous journey on the hippo, the excitement of seeing the world from such a great height, the soaring sensation of speed when they went to the city and saw Mr. Rumble's surprise—the enchanting Miss Tumble—then the perilous escape from the long angry arms when the miraculous pink carpet lifted him high, high in the air, and they sped off together where nothing could touch them.

Mr. Rumble had seemed disappointed to discover that Mr. Bumble just wanted to remember old times instead of doing something new, but the hippo said he understood and would come back when Mr. Bumble felt like going out again. As soon as the hippo was gone, Mr. Bumble remembered there was something he'd always wanted to ask him, but now he'd forgotten what it was. A moment later he was deep asleep and had even forgotten what it was he'd forgotten.

Sometimes when he was dozing in his mistress Jane's studio, she would put down her pieces of colored paper and come over and sit down beside him to talk. He didn't bother to listen, not because he didn't care, but because she always talked about the usual worries—was her work really worth it, what was she going to plant in her garden, were her family and friends healthy and happy, and what was she going to cook for dinner? But as familiar as all this was, Mr. Bumble could tell that lately something was different, something had changed inside him, because now when she gathered him up and hugged him and said, "Oh, Mr. Bumble, I just want this wonderful feeling to never end," he didn't try to wriggle out of her arms. He no longer even tried to pretend he didn't like it, because he did. He didn't want it to end either. Sometimes he even thought being held in her arms was better than any-thing—anything except the times when he stood on the floor in the kitchen and a piece of pork or chicken or turkey dropped from her hand and landed right in his bowl. Those were the things he lived for, food and sleep and lying in his mistress Jane's arms.

In the spring, when Mr. Grumble started digging the garden and his mistress Jane began planting seeds, Mr. Bumble was content to lie dozing nearby in the sun. He no longer helped with the digging, although sometimes he lay with his nose between his paws, watching.

When summer came and the garden began sprouting and blooming, his mistress Jane took him up and down the hay-covered paths and showed him all the kinds of tomatoes she was growing. "Brandywine and Purple Cherokee and Giant Belgium and Persimmon—and look at the zucchini and kale and all the garlic we're going to have!" Even Mr. Grumble got excited when he pointed out to Mr. Bumble the Delicata and Sweet Dumpling and Buttercup and Butternut and giant blue Hubbard squash growing among the vines. Mr. Bumble was glad the plants made them so happy, but since they never showed him a vine or a bush with pork or chicken or a dog biscuit growing on it, it didn't really matter to him what they grew.

In the fall, after most of the plants had been picked and eaten and the green stalks started turning brown, all the leaves began falling. His mistress Jane and Mr. Grumble spent hours raking the yard and piling the leaves in a heap where the pumpkins had been. Mr. Bumble watched them raking on the cool sunny afternoons but he no longer felt like chasing the leaves. Mr. Grumble tried to get him interested and once in a while, when a gust blew a leaf past his nose, he'd jump up before he knew what he was doing and run after it. If he caught it, he suddenly felt a bit foolish and wondered what he had wanted it for. When he sat down again he thought it was strange that once it had been so exciting to chase leaves and so important to catch them.

One day after all the leaves had fallen and the ground was starting to feel hard under his paws, his mistress Jane picked him up and carried him out to the car. That was one place he did not like at all. As they rode along, he could never fall asleep but always had to stand up on the seat to see where they were going because they usually went someplace he didn't want to go, like the kennel or the vet. Today it was the vet and, although the waiting room was empty, it smelled like a hundred dogs had just been there, and the powerful mixture of smells was alarming and confusing. Then they went into the room that Mr. Bumble was sure was dangerous because it was so full of odors he never smelled anywhere else, odors so strong and strange it made him afraid to take a deep breath. His mistress Jane lifted him up high and set him on a table so slippery she had to hold him so he wouldn't slide off on the floor. The vet put something cool on his chest, pulled open his mouth, looked in his eyes and ears, and squeezed and poked him all over.

"His heart and lungs still seem strong," said the vet, poking and prodding, "and he has some adipose tissue, which we'd expect at this age."

Mr. Bumble was sure the vet himself had some of that too, whatever it was. Then the fingers found the place on his side, the one that had started hurting a few days ago. It was the one place Mr. Bumble didn't want anyone to touch, most especially the vet.

"There's some swelling down here below the ribs and if you put your hand right here you can feel it. That's something we should watch. It could be serious."

Mr. Bumble had to struggle not to yelp while the vet's fingers probed and massaged the place on his side. Finally, the hand went away, and his mistress Jane picked him up and held him while she and the vet talked in voices that sounded as if something bad was going to happen. Mr. Bumble's only thought was to get out of this Room of Dangerous Odors, and even when they were finally back in the car he still didn't feel safe. She put him on the front seat, then picked him up again suddenly and said, "Oh, Mr. Bumble, I just don't want anything ever to hurt you!"

Mr. Bumble didn't want anything to hurt him either, and usually he felt safe when he was in his mistress Jane's arms. But now she was hugging him so tightly that the place on his side gave him a pain, a sharp bite, as if a tiny dog was biting him inside. He had to be very sure not to yelp, or she might take him right back in to see the vet again.

When they got home, he felt so tired all he wanted to do was take a nap. His mistress Jane gave him a biscuit; he ate it quickly, then lay down on his bed. Whatever it was that had been biting and gnawing inside him had stopped, but his side was still tender and he had to lie down on the opposite side in order to sleep.

That night when Mr. Grumble and his mistress Jane had their drinks, Mr. Bumble jumped up on the couch to lie down beside his mistress Jane. As he tried to doze, he kept hearing his name and knew they were talking about him. His mistress Jane was afraid that the thing biting inside him was her fault. "Last week in the kitchen, I kicked him," she said. "I was making dinner and stepped back to get something and he was right there on the floor. My foot went right into him. Maybe that's the same place the vet found."

"We've got to be careful," said Mr. Grumble. "He can't hear very well now, and he doesn't jump out of the way."

"Oh, I know," said his mistress Jane. "He's always right there while I'm cooking, hoping something will fall on the floor—and the way I rush around something usually does," she laughed and started stroking Mr. Bumble. "Will you forgive me? I didn't mean to hurt you. You know that, don't you?"

"I don't think that's what's wrong," said Mr. Grumble. "I felt something on his side, too, a few days ago, something swollen."

"Whatever it is, we have to keep checking it to make sure it doesn't get worse. The vet said the other choice is to have surgery to find out for sure what it is."

"No," said Mr. Grumble firmly, "we're not going to put the old guy through that."

The old guy, thought Mr. Bumble. That's what they're starting to call me. But he was only a little offended. Mostly he was just glad they weren't going to put him through something else at the vet's, and he dozed off with his mistress Jane stroking him.

Mr. Bumble began to feel better. The tiny invisible dog inside him stopped biting and he wasn't so tired, maybe because he didn't have to lie on only one side. He still wished he didn't have to take such long walks but it made his mistress Jane so happy when she looked down and saw him bumbling along on the end of the leash that he almost didn't mind. But strange things kept happening.

One Sunday morning when he lay on the end of the bed, Mr. Grumble started reading aloud descriptions of dogs in the newspaper. After a moment, his mistress Jane stopped him.

"That's terrible! You shouldn't be reading dog ads right in front of Mr. Bumble. How will that make him feel?"

"I'm just thinking someday we might want a bigger dog to protect you and Mr. Bumble when I'm away."

I may be old and I have been sick, thought Mr. Bumble, but no matter what, I would always protect my mistress Jane.

"Well, I don't want to get another dog as long as we have Mr. Bumble," she said. "That wouldn't be fair to him."

"No, you're right," said Mr. Grumble, throwing the newspaper on the floor. "After all this time, Mr. Bumble is used to being an Only Dog. Besides, he's going to live forever!"

"Oh, no, not forever," said his mistress Jane. "Who would take care of him if we weren't around?"

"Okay, not forever. Just another twenty years," said Mr. Grumble. "At least."

Mr. Bumble liked the sound of being an "Only Dog," but he also knew he wasn't going to last another twenty years; he couldn't walk that far, he thought with a shudder. But as long as he could sleep and eat and be hugged by his mistress Jane, he was glad to stay where he was and make them happy.

Winter came, and he went to the kennel for the visit that always happened soon after they brought a tree in the house and hung lights on it. When his mistress Jane came back a few days later to pick him up, she smelled like some dogs he'd never met. Usually this made him jealous, but this time he didn't really care. He just wanted to go home. The invisible dog had started gnawing on him again. Not all the time, but often enough, and although it bothered him, mostly he hoped his mistress Jane wouldn't notice. But as soon as they got home, she gave him such a strong hug that he had to hold his breath to keep from yelping.

"Are you all right, Mr. Bumble?" she asked. "Did they treat you well at the kennel? Does that lump on your side hurt?"

He felt her hand move down to the place the vet had found.

My side does hurt, he wanted to tell her, especially when she hugged him so hard or poked him. But he was glad she came back, and glad to be home again too.

Now they returned to their routine. After the last walk at night, his mistress Jane and Mr. Grumble went upstairs, and she took three small biscuits with her. Before starting up, Mr. Bumble paused at the bottom of the stairs because they got longer and steeper each time he climbed them. When he got near the top, he had to scramble to keep his paws from slipping out from under him. Upstairs, the bed was higher than ever too, and sometimes when he was standing there getting ready to jump, Mr. Bumble felt a hand slide under his belly and lift him up on the bed. He didn't really need the help, but he had reached the age when a little boost was only a small affront to his dignity.

Soon the tiny dog was gnawing inside him all the time. The only time Mr. Bumble didn't feel it was when he slept, so he tried to sleep as much as he could. While his mistress Jane and Mr. Grumble ate dinner, he curled up on his bed by the table and didn't even stay awake to see if her hand came down with a small piece of meat in it.

One strange winter evening, it was so warm and wet and foggy, it was almost like spring. When Mr. Grumble took him out for a walk before going to bed, the ground was spongy under his paws, and Mr. Bumble felt so weary he could barely carry himself out to the road. When he lifted his leg against the stone wall, the tiny invisible dog gave him an especially strong bite. He was ready for it and didn't yelp, but as Mr. Grumble led him down the road, he couldn't help dragging back on the leash.

"You want to go back, don't you," said Mr. Grumble. "I don't blame you. It's just the kind of night you'd expect the Hound of the Baskervilles to come bounding out of the field. We'll just walk down to the big rock and then come back."

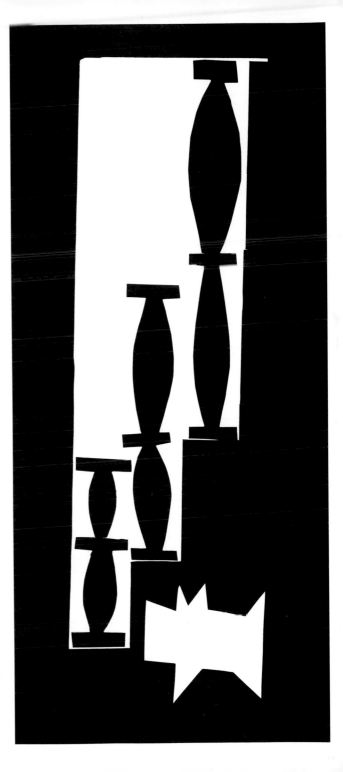

Mr. Bumble knew there was nothing to sniff down at the big rock, so he pulled at the leash and went off the road onto the cold wet grass. He took care of his personal business as fast as he could because, when he made the necessary effort, the tiny invisible dog bit him fiercely again.

Then he felt Mr. Grumble tugging the leash, pulling him back toward the road. But Mr. Bumble had gone far enough.

"Okay. I'm sorry," he heard Mr. Grumble say in the foggy dark. "Let's go home. I shouldn't be making you walk on such a bad night as this."

Mr. Bumble got up the stairs by himself but when his mistress Jane gave him a goodnight biscuit, he couldn't eat it. He held it in his teeth because, as bad as he felt, to give up a biscuit was against all his instinct. He finally set it down on the floor by the edge of the bed and, with a huge effort, jumped up by himself. As he lay down, his mistress Jane looked up from her book.

"Are you feeling all right, Mr. Bumble? I'm worried about you. I hope that place on your side isn't worse. Maybe it's just this strange weather we're having."

She reached down and stroked his head. He closed his eyes and she stroked him for a long time before she leaned back and picked up her book again.

Mr. Bumble's eyes were closed but he wasn't asleep. The tiny, invisible dog had clamped its jaws on something inside him so hard, he was sure this time he would yelp. If he did, his mistress Jane would know it wasn't just the strange weather tonight, and the next thing he knew he'd be in the Room of Dangerous Odors high up on the slippery table.

Then he felt her stroking his head very lightly again and Mr. Grumble started scratching his ears very gently while they agreed with each other that Mr. Bumble didn't feel very well tonight.

A few minutes later, he was lying very still on the bed when suddenly the invisible teeth let go.

Mr. Bumble's small body gave a great shudder.

Something inside him had broken, and now, all by itself, his body rose up and flopped over on his mistress Jane's legs so he was looking right into her eyes. But he couldn't see her. All he could see was a haze, a strange foggy haze.

When his mistress Jane felt Mr. Bumble flop on her legs—something he had never done before—she dropped her book and sat up quickly. She stared at him for an instant, then shouted to Mr. Grumble.

"Look—something's wrong! We've got to call the vet right away!"

Mr. Bumble felt their hands touching him on the swollen place and stroking his head, but now he didn't care if they called the vet. Even the Room of Dangerous Odors didn't frighten him.

His mistress Jane was dialing the telephone. "I got his machine!" she said. "Oh, why did this have to happen at night?"

"Look at his eyes," said Mr. Grumble. "They're so dilated. This is serious. Something's really wrong."

No, it isn't, Mr. Bumble wanted to tell them, *it's all right*. Because the bright foggy haze was now turning a soft pink and gray color and, as it slowly took shape, Mr. Bumble realized it was a hippo.

"How are you?" said Mr. Rumble. "I haven't seen you in quite a long time."

"I've grown old . . . very old," said Mr. Bumble, "and I haven't seen you because I've been sick. But I've missed you."

"I've missed you, too," said the hippo. "Shall we go for a walk?"

"I don't want to disappoint you," said Mr. Bumble, "but I'm just too tired to go for a walk. It's a wet foggy night, anyway."

"Don't worry about the weather," said the hippo, "and if you'd rather not walk, you can ride."

Mr. Bumble didn't want to admit it to Mr. Rumble, but he couldn't even stand up, so how could he jump up on the hippo's nose and climb up to his shoulders for a ride? But before Mr. Bumble could say anything, he felt himself rising up, and when he looked down he saw a long pink carpet under him. It curled high in the air, then he slowly slid down, and without moving a paw he found himself perched on the broad gray shoulders. For a moment, he was afraid he'd fall off, but they were already moving and all he had to do was just sit where he was as they glided through the haze.

As he peered through the haze, it was suddenly gone, and now Mr. Bumble and the hippo were soaring along. All around him, Mr. Bumble saw familiar places and the air was full of familiar smells. Things he had almost forgotten about passed by.

There were the Galloping Galoot and Attila the Pit Bull and Tyrannosaurus Taurus and Commander Bark towed along by his twin chows. All the big dogs who had frightened him so much now looked like pictures, the kind his mistress Jane made in her studio. They were all odd and curious bright-colored shapes that made people smile.

Mr. Bumble noticed the places soaring by too, all the places he had seen and sniffed and marked every day on his walks. Trees and rocks and hydrants and signs, the church and the post office, the field with Kate's sheep, the lawn where he and the hippo chased leaves, the heavenly yard where Miss Tumble ran through the thick grass in her silver-black coat with a single red rose on top of her head like a crown. And there was Werner's Pond where he had once said goodbye to his hippo. But now Mr. Rumble was right here with him, under his paws, and as they soared on together he looked down and saw a bright, sunlit garden full of tomatoes and corn and cucumbers and zucchini and lettuce and garlic and herbs and petunias and sunflowers—all the things his mistress Jane grew in her garden. Sitting in the middle of all these blooming and flowering things, he saw a woman with long golden-red hair streaming out from under a baseball cap. Her hands covered her face but, hearing the sound of her voice, he remembered the taste of tears on his tongue when he licked his mistress Jane's face, and knew who it was.

"What will I do without my dog?" she was crying. "Why did he have to leave me?"

"Mr. Rumble!" Mr. Bumble cried out to the hippo. "That's my mistress Jane! She's crying because she lost her dog. We have to go back and help her find him!"

"I'm afraid we can't go back," said Mr. Rumble. "Not this time."

"But she's so sad. I can't stand to hear her crying like that!"

"Don't worry," said Mr. Rumble. "She'll stop crying in a while."

"You mean when she finds her dog?"

"No," said Mr. Rumble. "That dog is gone."

"Gone? Is he lost?"

"They all get lost sometime," said Mr. Rumble. "Dogs don't last forever."

"I don't see why not," said Mr. Bumble. "Right now I feel as if I could last forever myself."

"Oh yes, indeed," agreed the hippo. "I do too."

"Even if we can't help her find her dog, I'd like to go back and tell my mistress Jane how much I loved her."

"Oh, she knows," said the hippo. "She knows."

"Why don't we just take her with us?" asked Mr. Bumble, who suddenly remembered he'd always wanted to find out where the hippo came from, so he added, "Wherever it is we're going."

"We can't," said Mr. Rumble.

"Why not?" asked Mr. Bumble.

"Because," explained Mr. Rumble, "you're someone who *once* was, and I'm someone who *never* was, and where we're going is a place that no one who *is* can ever go."

"I don't understand," said Mr. Bumble.

"It doesn't matter," said the hippo, "because now that you're someone who once was, you don't have to understand anything."

Indeed, Mr. Bumble did not understand anything.

As they soared farther and farther, he felt himself becoming lighter and lighter—as light as the hippo beneath him. Then, when he looked down, he saw that Mr. Rumble was gone too, and he was soaring all by himself. It was such a wonderful feeling, he wished his mistress Jane could feel it too. Because he knew if she did, she'd stop crying and be as happy as he was, even if he would never bumble along behind her again.

Jimmy
(aka Mr. Bumble)
with Jane and Bill
1990

Bill Wheatley and Jane Duderstadt have both worked as producers for public television in Boston. They now live in a village in rural Massachusetts where he continues work in production and she paints and runs Jane's Heritage Tomatoes in season. They also take walks with Murdo, Mr. Bumble's successor, and Bix, an Airedale.